J 975.9 Ham
Hamalainen, Karina,
Everglades /
$31.00   on1020293219

SM   OCT 0 3 2018

Y0-CKM-482

3 4028 10004 8264
HARRIS COUNTY PUBLIC LIBRARY

WITHDRAW

National Parks
Everglades

KARINA HAMALAINEN

Children's Press®
An Imprint of Scholastic Inc.

Content Consultant
James Gramann, PhD
Professor Emeritus, Department of Recreation, Park and Tourism Sciences
Texas A&M University, College Station, Texas

Library of Congress Cataloging-in-Publication Data
Names: Hamalainen, Karina, author.
Title: Everglades / by Karina Hamalainen.
Description: New York, NY : Children's Press, an imprint of Scholastic Inc., 2019. | Series: A true book | Includes bibliographical references and index.
Identifiers: LCCN 2018002252 | ISBN 9780531175927 (library binding) | ISBN 9780531189979 (pbk.)
Subjects: LCSH: Everglades National Park (Fla.)—Juvenile literature.Classification: LCC F317.E9 H356 2019 | DDC 975.9/39—dc23
LC record available at https://lccn.loc.gov/2018002252

No part of this publication may be reproduced in whole or in part, or stored in a retrieval system, or transmitted in any form or by any means, electronic, mechanical, photocopying, recording, or otherwise, without written permission of the publisher. For information regarding permission, write to Scholastic Inc., Attention: Permissions Department, 557 Broadway, New York, NY 10012.
© 2019 Scholastic Inc.

All rights reserved. Published in 2019 by Children's Press, an imprint of Scholastic Inc.
Printed in Heshan, China 62

SCHOLASTIC, CHILDREN'S PRESS, A TRUE BOOK™, and associated logos are trademarks and/or registered trademarks of Scholastic Inc.

Scholastic Inc., 557 Broadway, New York, NY 10012

1 2 3 4 5 6 7 8 9 10 R 28 27 26 25 24 23 22 21 20 19

Front cover (main): Airboat
Front cover (inset): American crocodile
Back cover: American white pelican

Find the Truth!

Everything you are about to read is true *except* for one of the sentences on this page.

Which one is **TRUE**?

T or F The most common plant in Everglades National Park is saw grass.

T or F An alligator's snout has a pointy shape, like the letter A.

Find the answers in this book.

Contents

1 A Watery World
How did the Everglades become a national park? 7

2 Exploring the Park
What kinds of environments are found in the park? 13

3 Amazing Animals
What different animals live in the park? 19

THE BIG TRUTH!

National Parks Field Guide: Everglades
What animals will you see in the Everglades? 26

Alligator

A walkway above Shark Valley

4 Parade of Plants
What unique plants grow in the park? 29

5 Protecting the Park
How will the park look in the next 10 years? 35

Map Mystery 40
Be an Animal Tracker! 42
True Statistics 44
Resources 45
Important Words 46
Index 47
About the Author 48

Snail kite

The Wilderness Waterway is a 99-mile (159-kilometer) trail that visitors can explore only by boat.

CHAPTER

A Watery World

It takes a week to paddle your canoe through the swamps of Everglades National Park to Flamingo, at the southern tip of Florida. During your trip through the **wetlands**, you see alligators and crocodiles relaxing in the sun. A manatee nibbles on seagrass. A golden orb weaver spider builds its giant web. You arrive just in time for sunset. Despite the itchy mosquito bites you picked up along the way, it's been an amazing adventure!

Everglades National Park

Wondrous Wetlands

The Everglades is the country's largest **subtropical** wetlands. It once covered the southern two-thirds of Florida. As a **drainage basin**, the area's precipitation drains into Lake Okeechobee and on to Florida Bay. Florida is flat, so the water drains slowly.

The Calusa were the largest group of people in the area up to the 1500s. They ventured into the Everglades to hunt and fish.

Timeline of the Everglades

1000 BCE
The Calusa society forms in the Everglades. They make art and shell tools.

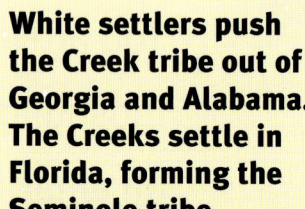

1513
Spanish explorer Juan Ponce de León arrives on Easter. He names Florida after the Spanish name for Easter, *Pascua Florida* (Feast of Flowers).

1700s
White settlers push the Creek tribe out of Georgia and Alabama. The Creeks settle in Florida, forming the Seminole tribe.

Changes in the Everglades

The Calusa and other groups were mostly wiped out by European explorers in the 16th century. In the 1700s, the Creek tribe arrived. Joining other Native Americans and escaped slaves, they became the Seminoles. The U.S. government fought the Seminoles for years. By the mid-1800s, most had died or moved to Oklahoma. But about 300 stayed. Their descendants still live in the Everglades.

1817–1858
The Seminole Wars take place. General (and future president) Andrew Jackson tries to remove the Seminoles from Florida.

1905
The Florida governor orders projects to drain the Everglades so farms and towns can be built.

1947
President Harry Truman dedicates Everglades National Park on December 6.

Marjory Stoneman Douglas called the Everglades the "River of Grass."

Taming the Swamp

Toward the end of the 19th century, Americans wanted to farm and live farther south in Florida. But the Everglades were too wet. Starting in 1905, the government drained the wetlands.

With more dry land for farming, the population boomed. But the lack of flowing water spelled trouble for the Everglades **ecosystem**. Beginning in the 1930s, environmentalist Marjory Stoneman Douglas wrote about the Everglades. Her work encouraged people to protect the land as a national park. On December 6, 1947, President Harry Truman dedicated the park.

National Park Fact File

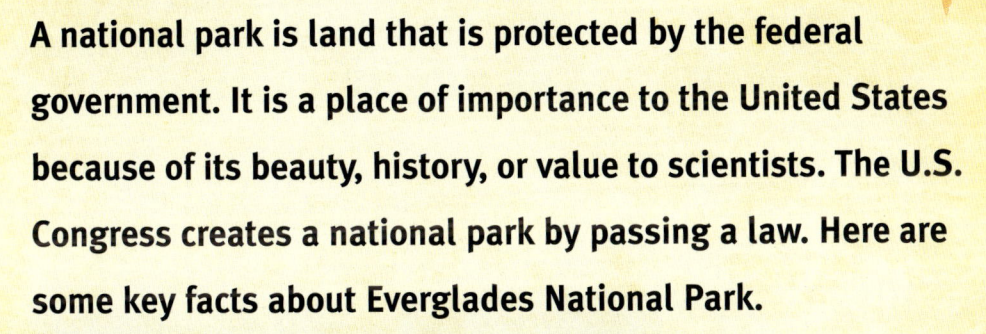

A national park is land that is protected by the federal government. It is a place of importance to the United States because of its beauty, history, or value to scientists. The U.S. Congress creates a national park by passing a law. Here are some key facts about Everglades National Park.

Everglades National Park	
Location	Southern Florida
Year established	1947
Size	2,357 square miles (6,105 sq km), about the same size as Delaware
Average number of visitors each year	1 million
Location of highest viewpoint for visitors	Shark Valley Observation Tower, at 65 feet (20 m)
Longest boat trail	Wilderness Waterway at 99 miles (159 km), nearly as much as Hawai'i, the country's wettest state
Average annual rainfall	60 inches (152.4 centimeters)

An elevated walkway stretches over Shark Valley, giving visitors a view of the swamp from the treetops.

12

CHAPTER 2

Exploring the Park

Everglades National Park is the only subtropical park in the continental United States. That means it is very warm and very, very wet. The park is home to plants and animals that can't be seen anywhere else in the country. Although the Everglades are best known as a swamp, there are several different ecosystems in the park. Visitors can go canoeing through the wetlands, spend a day on the sandy beaches, or hike through the forests.

With heavy rainfall, most of the Everglades are underwater for part or all of the year.

What a Swamp!

A great place to start an Everglades adventure is Shark Valley. A fan-powered airboat can whisk passengers through the sloughs (SLOOZ). Sloughs have small rivers that run between teardrop-shaped islands of plant life.

Visitors can also hike or bike along paved roads. A 65-foot-tall (20-meter) tower along the way gives a bird's-eye view of the sloughs.

Wetland Words

Wetlands are areas that are permanently or seasonally covered with water. There are different names for different kinds of wetlands in the Everglades.

SWAMP
Wetlands with forests

MARSH
Wetlands with many leafy plants

SLOUGH
Partially muddy wetlands that connect to larger bodies of water

Cypress "knees" grow around the trees' roots. The knees might send air to underwater roots, but no one knows for sure!

From here, you can also explore the cypress domes. A cypress dome is where many cypress trees grow together. The trees in the center are taller than those on the edges. This gives the cluster a round shape, like a dome. If you don't mind getting wet and muddy, you can hike through the cypress swamp. This type of wetlands hiking is called slogging.

Fantastic Forests

Although the Everglades are generally very flat, there are forests to explore at higher **elevations**. In the pinelands ecosystem, hard rocks are near the surface. It's a mostly open area with tall, skinny pine trees and low plants. You'll find shade in the hardwood hammocks. These are forests of leafy hardwood trees such as mahogany and oak. Visitors can spot larger animals here, such as deer and panthers. Plants such as ferns and orchids grow in the shade.

There are 19,840 acres (8,029 hectares) of pine forests in the park.

People can camp by the islands on wooden platforms called chickees.

Ten Thousand Islands

Freshwater meets the sea in the **estuarine** ecosystem. Along the west and south coasts are many tiny islands. Though the region is called Ten Thousand Islands, the actual number is a few hundred. Some islands, called keys, are the tops of old coral reefs. Others are formed by mangrove trees that have grown densely together.

CHAPTER  3

Amazing Animals

No matter which part of the park you visit, you will see many animals. Small mammals scurry through the forests. Hundreds of fish swim through the water. Look up! You'll see flocks of birds flying overhead. There are also millions of insects—including some that bite, such as mosquitoes. Each ecosystem is home to different animals.

 Like the flamingo, the roseate spoonbill gets its stunning pink coloring from the food it eats.

Wet and Wild

More than 300 species of freshwater and saltwater fish live in the Everglades' waterways. If you're older than 16, you'll need to get a license to go fishing. Otherwise, you can go without a license. You could reel in a redfish, snapper, barracuda, channel catfish, or bluegill. Keep an eye out for manatees and dolphins, too, and be careful not to hurt these protected species. Five of the world's seven species of sea turtles have also been spotted here.

Great barracudas swim at up to 35 miles (56 km) per hour when attacking prey.

Manatee or Mermaid?

When Christopher Columbus first spotted a manatee in 1493, he thought it was a mermaid! Also known as "sea cows," manatees spend about eight hours each day grazing on seagrass. They prefer the shallow waters where rivers meet the sea. About 5,000 manatees live in south Florida. But many of these gentle mammals have died and others have been scarred from being accidentally hit by the propellers of motorboats.

Though now only in Florida, Florida panthers once lived across much of the southeastern United States.

Landlubbers

Although there isn't much dry land in the Everglades, there is enough to support many different creatures. About 100 Florida panthers hunt for white-tailed deer in the hardwood hammocks. Nocturnal animals such as bats and opossums roam the park at night. At the edges of the land and water, frogs and toads sing a chorus. You'll hear the chirping of the bird-voiced tree frog or the "briiiiiiiiip" of the southern toad.

Alligators Versus Crocodiles

The only place in the country where both alligators and crocodiles live is the Everglades. Alligators live across the southeastern United States. Florida is the southernmost part of their range. Crocodiles typically live farther south in the world. The Everglades are the farthest north they can be found.

Gator or Croc?
Here's how you can tell alligators and crocodiles apart.

Feature	Crocodile	Alligator
Color	Grayish green	Blackish green
Snout shape	Pointy like the letter A	Rounded like the letter U
Teeth	Teeth on lower jaw are exposed when its mouth is closed	Teeth on upper jaw are exposed when its mouth is closed
Habitat	Prefers salt water	Prefers fresh water

Crocodile

Alligator

Florida is the only place in the United States where snail kites, a type of bird of prey, are found.

Birds of Paradise

Bird watchers flock to the Everglades! Many bird species live in the park year-round. Others, such as geese, ducks, and American oystercatchers, migrate here to enjoy the warm winter.

There are 16 types of wading birds in the park. Herons, egrets, and roseate spoonbills have long legs to walk through water. Their long beaks catch fish or other water creatures. Meanwhile, birds of prey such as osprey, snail kites, and turkey vultures soar through the air.

Don't Forget the Bug Spray!

Wherever there's water, there are insects. Many insects need water to lay their eggs. Although mosquitoes are the park's most famous insects, more than 1,000 other types of bugs have been spotted here. Butterflies float through the air looking for flowers. Dragonflies zoom over the water. Many kinds of arthropods live here, too. Millipedes and centipedes scurry through the leaves. And watch out for spider webs! The golden orb weaver's web can be more than 3 feet (1 m) wide.

One scientist on nearby Sanibel Island caught 365,696 mosquitoes in one night!

THE BIG TRUTH!

National Parks Field Guide: Everglades

Here are a few of the hundreds of fascinating animals you may see in the park.

American white pelican

Scientific name: *Pelecanus erythrorhynchos*

Habitat: Winters in inland wetlands; summers are spent farther north

Diet: Fish and aquatic organisms

Fact: With a wingspan of more than 8.3 feet (2.5 m), it is one of the largest birds in the United States.

Redfish

Scientific name: *Sciaenops ocellatus*

Habitat: Coasts, river mouths, and bays along the Atlantic and Gulf of Mexico

Diet: Small crustaceans, such as crabs and shrimp, and small fish

Fact: Also called the red drum, it makes a drumming sound by vibrating a muscle in its abdomen.

Loggerhead sea turtle

Scientific name: *Caretta caretta*

Habitat: Warmer ocean waters

Diet: Jellyfish, conchs, crabs, fish, and occasionally seaweed and algae

Fact: Every two years, female loggerhead turtles travel up to 7,450 miles (11,990 km) back to the beaches where they were born to lay their eggs.

Peninsula newt

Scientific name: *Notophthalmus viridescens piaropicola*

Habitat: Freshwater canals, lakes, and ponds

Diet: Small crustaceans, fish and amphibian eggs, and insect larvae (young insects)

Fact: Peninsula newts navigate, or find their way around, using Earth's magnetic field.

Bobcat

Scientific name: *Lynx rufus*

Habitat: Woodlands and swamps

Diet: Small mammals, birds, and fish

Fact: You can spot bobcat scat, or feces, along the park's trails by the fur and bones in it.

Northern yellow bat

Scientific name: *Lasiurus intermedius*

Habitat: Wooded areas near coastal habitats with palm trees

Diet: Insects such as mosquitoes, beetles, grasshoppers, and flying ants

Fact: Their yellow-gray color helps the bats hide out in dried palm fronds.

CHAPTER

Parade of Plants

More than 750 different plant species are native to the park. But the most common plant in the Everglades is saw grass. This grass-like plant is the key species in the freshwater marshes that cover most of the Everglades. These marshes are sometimes called glades, giving the park its name. To the first European visitors, the glades looked like they went on forever. So they combined the words "ever" and "glade" to name it.

 One in three Floridians relies on Everglades National Park for his or her water supply.

Elevation Matters

The Everglades are mostly flat. But even a few inches of change in elevation can make a big difference in which plants grow. They range from magnificent mangroves to microscopic algae. Algae are tiny organisms that use the sun to create energy. In groups of algae, bacteria and **decomposing** particles combine to create periphyton (puh-RIF-ih-tuhn). This living mud floats on rivers and swamps in sausage-shaped tubes. It also attaches to underwater surfaces such as mangrove tree roots and riverbeds.

Don't touch the saw grass! Its edges have tiny supersharp "teeth" that can cut you.

Plants Through the Park

Pineland Forests
This area is home to pine trees, palm trees, and leafy plants.

Slash pines

Hardwood Hammocks
Hardwood trees, leafy plants, ferns, and orchids grow here.

Orchids

Cypress Domes
Cypress trees, leafy plants, ferns, and various flowers live in this ecosystem.

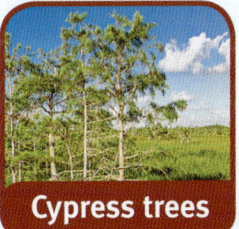
Cypress trees

Mangrove Forests
Mangrove trees give this ecosystem its name. The area is also home to leafy plants.

Mangrove tree

Marine & Estuarine
Seagrasses and algae grow in this water environment.

Mermaid's wine glass algae

Coastal Prairie
This land, wet with salt water, nourishes salt-tolerant shrubs and small, fleshy plants called succulents.

Grasses

Sloughs
Freshwater marine plants are found underwater. Tall grasses, saw grass, and other leafy plants also grow here.

Saltwort

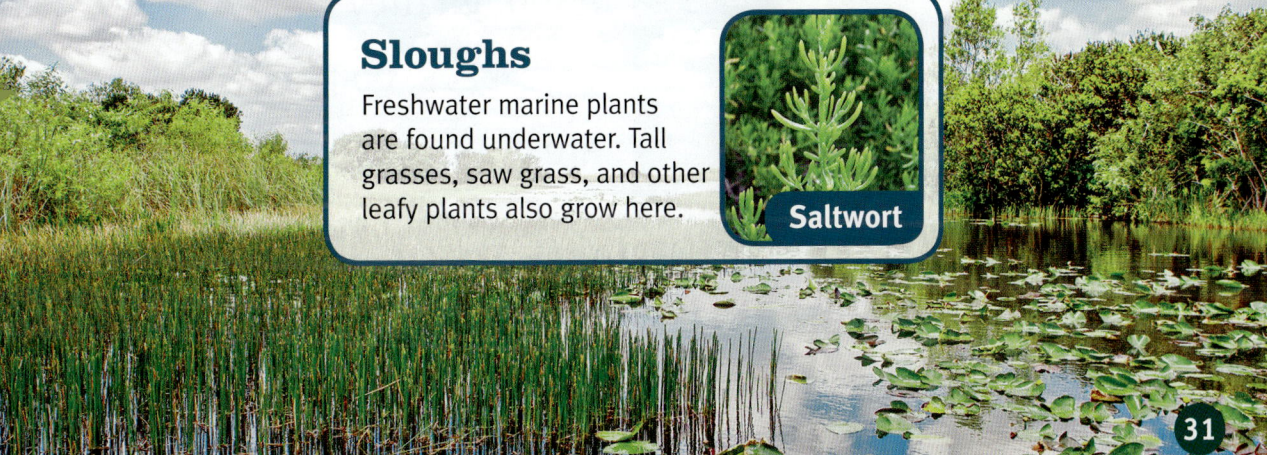

Sky-High Plants

Throughout the Everglades, you will see curtains of Spanish moss draped across tree branches. It's one of the many plants here that don't grow on the ground or in the water. Also known as epiphytes, these plants get nutrients and water from the air. For this reason, they are nicknamed air plants. Some orchid species are also epiphytes. Although they latch onto trees, epiphytes are not parasites and do not harm the trees.

Epiphytes are most common in warm, moist places.

Outrageous Orchids

Orchids provide bursts of color in the park. Orchid flowers come in a rainbow of colors. They also range in size from the jingle bell that fits in your hand to the foot-tall cowhorn. It's illegal to remove plants from the park. But some people break the law. At least three orchid species are now extinct in the Everglades because humans took too many of them.

With 39 native species, the Everglades have the greatest diversity of orchids in the country.

Different park rangers have different responsibilities. Some enforce park rules. Others teach the public.

CHAPTER 5

Protecting the Park

Many laws protect national parks. But even the actions of people outside the park have serious effects on the Everglades. Projects to dry up Florida's land have changed how the water flows through the wetlands. Development and agriculture have also taken their toll. That's why the U.S. Congress approved the Comprehensive Everglades Restoration Plan in 2000. Over the coming years, the government plans to spend up to $8 billion to restore and protect the Everglades ecosystem.

Hunters shake hands after successfully catching a python in the Everglades.

Some experts estimate that as many as 300,000 pythons live in the Everglades.

Python Problem

Burmese pythons are originally from Asia. But in the Everglades, they are an invasive species. For years, these giant snakes either escaped from or were intentionally released by people who tried to raise them as pets but found them too challenging. Now the snakes have taken over the park. Pythons eat anything—even alligators! This leaves less food for native species. The state has hired hunters to catch the invasive snakes.

Wild Weather

Hurricane season in the Atlantic is from June through November. Every few years, a major hurricane passes through the Everglades. In 2017, Hurricane Irma caused devastating damage. It tore up trees and flooded many parts of the region for months. Scientists warn that **climate change** can cause these superstorms to happen more frequently. Low-lying lands like the Everglades are under threat from a rise in sea levels as global temperatures increase.

A tree destroyed by Hurricane Irma blocks a Miami road in 2017.

Chemicals used to control plants outside the park can enter parklands through runoff.

Poisonous Pollution

Agricultural **runoff** from nearby farms finds its way into the park. Fertilizer in the runoff causes plants and algae to grow too much. It also allows non-native plants such as cattails to take root. The Everglades soil used to be too poor for these plants to grow. Now there are too many of them.

Air pollution is also a problem. Heavy metals such as mercury are in the air and fall down with rain. Mercury can harm animals' health and development.

Water Woes

The wetlands act like a giant filter to clean water before it's stored in **aquifers** deep below the earth. But it's a slow process. As more people move to South Florida, they use up more water. If people remove too much, the aquifers could run dry or fill up with undrinkable salt water. That's another reason behind the Everglades restoration plan. Everyone must work together to make sure the park remains healthy for years to come! ★

In drier areas, cypress trees do not grow as tall. These shorter trees are called "dwarf cypresses."

Map Mystery

What's one of the best bird-watching destinations in Everglades National Park? Follow the directions below to find the answer.

Directions

1. Start at the Shark Valley Visitor Center at the north end of the park.

2. Travel west to the island of Chokoloskee to launch your boat into the water.

3. Take the Wilderness Waterway southeast to North River Chickee. There, you'll camp the night on the chickee's elevated platform.

4. Head due south to the town of Flamingo. It's the southernmost point in the park and in mainland Florida.

5. Follow the road northeast to the trailhead. This is the start of the trail you're looking for. Don't forget your binoculars!

Everglades National Park

Key to Ecosystems
- Marine and Estuarine
- Coastal Marsh
- Mangrove
- Cypress
- Coastal Prairie
- Freshwater Slough
- Pineland
- Freshwater Marl Prairie
- Hardwood Hammock

Labels on map:
- FLORIDA
- Gulf Coast Visitor Center
- Chokoloskee
- Big Cypress Swamp Welcome Center
- BIG CYPRESS NATIONAL PRESERVE
- Shark Valley Visitor Center
- Ten Thousand Islands
- Wilderness Waterway
- GULF OF MEXICO
- Tram Trail
- Observation Tower
- Ernest F. Coe Visitor Center
- North River Chickee
- Main Park Road
- Royal Palm Anhinga Trail
- Flamingo
- Flamingo Visitor Center
- FLORIDA BAY
- ATLANTIC OCEAN

Compass Rose: North, South, East, West

U.S. Area of map
Alaska and Hawai'i are not drawn to scale or placed in their proper places.

Answer: Royal Palm Anhinga Trail

41

Be an Animal Tracker!

If you're ever in the Everglades, keep an eye out for these animal tracks. They'll help you know which animals are in the area.

Florida panther
Paw length: 3 inches (7.6 cm)

Bobcat
Paw length: 2 inches (5 cm)

River otter
Paw length: 3.25 inches (8.3 cm)

Opossum
Paw length: 1.5 inches (3.8 cm)

White-tailed deer
Hoof length: 4 inches (10 cm)

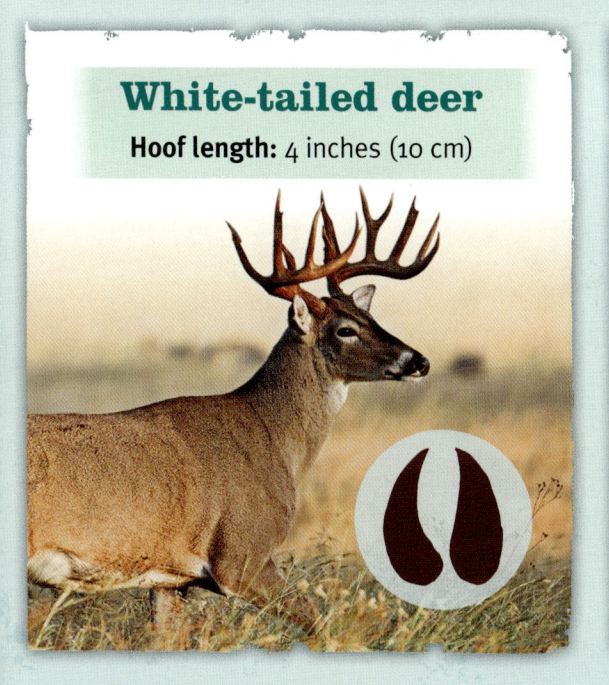

Marsh rabbit
Front paw length: 1 inch (2.5 cm)

43

True Statistics

Highest elevation: 8 ft. (2.4 m)
Number of mammal species in the park: 40
Number of bird species: 360
Number of amphibian and reptile species: 77
Number of fish species: More than 300
Number of insect and other arthropod species: More than 1,000
Number of plant species: More than 750
Total number of endangered species: 13
Percent of the Everglades ecosystem included in the national park: 20

Did you find the truth?

T The most common plant in Everglades National Park is saw grass.

F An alligator's snout has a pointy shape, like the letter A.

Resources

Books

Flynn, Sarah Wassner, and Julie Beer. *National Parks Guide U.S.A.* Washington, DC: National Geographic, 2016.

Marsico, Katie. *The Everglades*. Ann Arbor, MI: Cherry Lake Publishing, 2013.

Visit this Scholastic website for more information on Everglades National Park:
★ www.factsfornow.scholastic.com
Enter the keyword **Everglades**

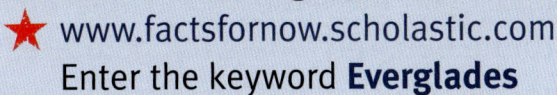

Important Words

aquifers (AK-wih-furz) layers of rock, sand, or gravel that contain water

climate change (KLYE-mit CHAYNJ) global warming and other changes in the weather and weather patterns that are happening because of human activity

decomposing (dee-kuhm-POZE-ing) rotting or decaying

drainage basin (DRAY-nij BAY-sihn) the region or land area that drains into a river, lake, or ocean

ecosystem (EE-koh-sis-tuhm) all the living things in a place and their relation to their environment

elevations (el-uh-VAY-shuhnz) heights above sea level

estuarine (ESS-choo-air-in) relating to an area where fresh water connects to the open ocean

runoff (RUN-awf) water from rain or snow that drains from an area of land and often carries pollution

subtropical (suhb-TRAH-pih-kuhl) region near the tropics (areas close to the equator) where temperatures rarely go below freezing and where plants can grow year-round

wetlands (WET-landz) land where there is a lot of moisture in the soil

Index

Page numbers in **bold** indicate illustrations.

alligators, **23**, 36
aquifers, 39

bats, 22, **27**
birds, **18**, 19, **24**, **26**
bobcats, **27**, **42**

chickees, **17**
climate, 11, 13, **37**
crocodiles, 7, **23**
cypress domes, 15, 31

deer, 16, 22, **43**
development, 9, 35
Douglas, Marjory Stoneman, **10**
draining, 8, 9, 10, 35

elevation, 11, 16, 30
establishment, 9, 10, 11
estuarine ecosystem, 17, **31**
exploration, 8, 9, 29

farming, 9, 10, 35, 38
fish, 8, 19, **20**, 24, **26**
Florida Bay, 8

grasses, 14, 21, 29, **30**, **31**

hardwood hammock, 16, 22, 31
hurricanes, **37**

insects, 19, **25**
islands, 17

keys, 17

Lake Okeechobee, 8

manatees, 20, **21**
mangrove trees, 17, 30, **31**
maps, **7**, 40–**41**
marine ecosystem, 17, **31**
marshes, **14**, 29

Native Americans, **8**, 9

opossums, 22, **43**
orchids, 16, 31, 32, **33**

panthers, 16, **22**, **42**
periphyton, 30
Pinelands, **16**, **31**
pollution, **38**
pythons, **36**

rangers, **34**
redfish, 20, **26**
roseate spoonbills, **18**, 19, 24

saw grass, 14, 29, **30**
sea turtles, 20, **27**
Shark Valley, 11, **12**, 14
sloughs, 14, **31**

timeline, **8**–**9**
tourism, **6**, 11, **12**, 13, 14, **17**
trails, **6**, 11, **12**
trees, **12**, **15**, 16, 17, 30, **31**, **32**, **37**
Truman, Harry, 9, 10

water, 8, 10, 17, 25, **28**, 29, 35, 39
Wilderness Waterway, **6**, 11

About the Author

Karina Hamalainen has been a writer and editor of Scholastic's science and math magazines for eight years. Today, she is the executive editor of *Scholastic MATH*, a magazine that connects current events to the math that students are learning in middle school. She's written stories about everything from the science of *Star Trek* to the effects of the *Deepwater Horizon* oil spill on the Gulf of Mexico. She lives in New York City, and tries to escape the city and explore the wilderness often!

PHOTOGRAPHS ©: cover main: Sylvain Grandadam/Robert Harding Picture Library; cover inset: Carlton Ward/Getty Images; back cover: imageBROKER/Superstock, Inc.; 3: Duncan McNicol/Getty Images; 4: blickwinkel/Alamy Images; 5 top: Rachel Bert/age fotostock; 5 bottom: James Urbach/Superstock, Inc.; 6: James H. Robinson/Science Source; 8 left: The Granger Collection; 8 center: The Granger Collection; 8 right: State Archives of Florida/Florida Memory/Alamy Images; 9 left: MPI/Getty Images; 9 center: The Granger Collection; 9 right: Jay Yuan/Shutterstock; 10: Orlando Sentinel/Getty Images; 11: Stephen Saks Photography/Alamy Images; 12: Rachel Bert/age fotostock; 14 left: James Schwabel/Alamy Images; 14 center: Steven Greaves/Getty Images; 14 right: NPS Photo/Alamy Images; 15: Yobro10/iStockphoto; 16: Tim Laman/National Geographic/Superstock, Inc.; 17: Tim Laman/Getty Images; 18: imageBROKER/Superstock, Inc.; 20: Pete Oxford/Minden Pictures/Superstock, Inc.; 21: Ron and Valerie Taylor/Pantheon/Superstock, Inc.; 22: Mark Conlin/Getty Images; 23 left: Joel Sartore/Getty Images; 23 right: blickwinkel/Alamy Images; 24: James Urbach/Superstock, Inc.; 25: Greg Lovett/The Palm Beach Post/ZUMAPRESS.com/Alamy Images; 26-27 background: Nagel Photography/Shutterstock; 26 bottom left: blickwinkel/Alamy Images; 26 bottom right: Michelson, Robert S/Animals Animals; 27 top left: Mark Conlin/Superstock, Inc.; 27 top right: Joel Sartore/Getty Images; 27 bottom left: CORDIER Sylvain/hemis.fr/Hemis/Superstock, Inc.; 27 bottom right: Michael Durham/Minden Pictures; 28: Juan Carlos Munoz/Minden Pictures; 30: RosaIreneBetancourt 6/Alamy Images; 31 background: Romrodphoto/Shutterstock; 31 top left: Tom Salyer/Alamy Images; 31 top right: Edwin Remsberg/age fotostock/Superstock, Inc.; 31 center top left: James Schwabel/Alamy Images; 31 center top right: Jon E Oringer/Shutterstock; 31 center bottom left: Brian Parker/Alamy Images; 31 center bottom right: RosaIreneBetancourt 12/Alamy Images; 31 bottom: Tom Salyer/Alamy Images; 32: Ingo Arndt/Minden Pictures/Superstock, Inc.; 33: Mike Booth/Alamy Images; 34: ullstein bild/Getty Images; 36: Michael Freifeld/Alamy Images; 37: Joe Raedle/Getty Images; 38: Aurora Photos/Alamy Images; 39: Ingo Arndt/Minden Pictures; 42-43 animal tracks: Natarto76/Shutterstock; 42 left: Mark Conlin/Getty Images; 42 right: CORDIER Sylvain/hemis.fr/Hemis/Superstock, Inc.; 43 top left: NHPA/Superstock, Inc.; 43 top right: Konrad Wothe/Minden Pictures/Superstock, Inc.; 43 bottom left: Danita Delimont/Getty Images; 43 bottom right: Daniela Duncan/Getty Images; 43 rabbit track: Natarto76/Shutterstock; 44: Joel Sartore/Getty Images.

Maps by Bob Italiano.

Harris County Public Library, Houston, TX